THE COMING OF TALLIS

Published in Canada by Engen Books, St. John's, NL.

ISBN-13: 978-1-77478-071-8

Distributed by:
Engen Books
www.engenbooks.com
submissions@engenbooks.com

First mass market paperback printing: November 2021

Cover Design: Ellen Curtis

Slipstreamers Committee:
Amanda Labonté
Ali House
AJ Ryan
Ellen Curtis
Erin Vance
Lauralana Dunne
Matthew LeDrew

THE COMING OF TALLIS

MATTHEW LEDREW & JD RYOT

CHAPTER ONE

Cassidy Cane ran from the laser fire with a big smile on her face, even though some of it was close enough to pass through her jacket and make sizzling holes in it. Despite the danger, her blood was pumping. In her hand she had clasped the Amulet of Zeus, one of the ten fabled Amulets of the Ok'Tid. Only one still existed on her world, with the rest lost to history, but on this world the population had found a way to perfectly preserve artifacts.

She had been looking for a way to copy that technology for use on her adventures, both at home and on other worlds, but then she had seen the Amulet and something about it had called to her and she had just had to touch it. She had felt that blood pumping in her ears and the smile had grown on her cheeks and she had just needed to have her hand against it. It looked so new here, not like the one she'd seen back home.

The moment her skin had connected with it alarms had started to go off, and all the faces in the museum she'd been visiting turned and glared at her as one, as though they were a hive mind.

"I guess that's the end of that," she'd said. Her voice was resigned but she had not been able to quell the smile growing across her lips. She had gripped her hand around the artifact almost instinctively, and when she had turned to run, she ran with it.

As she watched, the people of this dimension turned their heads and followed her, then quickly transformed into cat people. Their noses and mouths came together in snouts and they grew hair quickly, as though it had been waiting under the skin for the chance to emerge all this time. They hissed, raised their laser weapons, and started after her.

They fired at her again, and she felt a hot beam whiz past her neck so close that it tanned it. Despite the fear she should have been feeling, the blood was pumping in her so hard that she could feel it in her earlobes and in her fingers, and she smiled broadly and honestly.

She rounded a corner into a corridor that seemed to have no exit and started down it quickly.

The cat people turned around the same corner less than thirty seconds later in hot pursuit, but they found it empty. There was no trace of Cassidy Cane, or the Amulet of Zeus. The lead guard lowered its brow, curled its lip, and hissed. "Slipstreamer."

***

Preston Cane sat on the park bench alone. Even though there were no people with him – not his wife or any of his daughters – he didn't feel alone. He had his bag of bird-seed with him, and pigeons had flocked to his feet to take his gift. Some days, when the sun was hot and the breeze was good, they were all the company he needed.

"Hello," said a man with black hair and a slender face. He sat down on the bench next to Preston and set a sack lunch between them. "Mind if I join you?"

Preston turned and looked at him, shocked out of his train of thought for a moment. "Absolutely not; to each their own."

The man nodded, then reached into his bag and pulled out two halves of a sandwich. He handed one to Preston. "Cucumber sandwich?"

Preston eyed it hungrily. "That's my favourite."

"Take it, then."

Preston took the half gratefully, and both men started eating. "I'm Preston, by the way," he said, extending his free hand.

The man took it. "Tallis."

CHAPTER TWO

The Plainsfield Mall was one of those standard two-floor mall layouts that seemed to come standard with every town in America of over 50,000 residents. It was long and flat and took up far too much acreage for the benefits it provided. Despite how large it was, most of the space was taken up by wide halls: except the top floor, which had ninety percent of its middle carved out so that pedestrians could look down and see the patrons and storefronts below.

Cassidy stepped past a trendy outwear shop towards the food court in the heart of the building, bypassing adults and children as she did. She eyed a bomber jacket on a window-displayed mannequin that looked startlingly like the one she wore, but without the barrage of holes, and considered it. Seeing it in its 'complete' state made her suddenly aware of the state that her own had gotten into over the course of the last year. There were tears from getting caught in the thorns of plants on other worlds. There were bullet holes from fire she'd barely evaded. There were places where the fabric had gone rough from going from extreme hot to extreme cold too quickly, between portals. She wore the history of her adventures along her shoulders, she realized, and though the new coat made her realize how ripped and torn her current one was, she smiled and wore those tears with pride.

She eyed the jacket just once more, then continued on deeper into the mall. It was filled with people today, and she could already see the glut of them sitting at the food court. There were so many that she couldn't tell one from the other. She knew that Rica was amongst them some-where though, and from the last text she'd gotten, she'd already nabbed a clean seat and was waiting for her.

Frederica was nineteen and in all those years she had never once been called by her full name by someone close enough to have known her, as far as Cassidy could re-member. She had always been Rica. Whenever her full name, Frederica, had been said over the loudspeaker at school it had always taken her a moment to realize they were talking to her. It was a name that sounded foreign to her ear, despite being technically hers. Of Cassidy's two sisters, Rica was the quieter of the two. She hadn't graduated yet, but was planning on attending Plainsfield University when she did, and had politely asked Cassidy not to put herself into the process, one way or the other. Cassidy had respected that. Soon it would be that time, and Cassidy was anxious to see the result.

Months ago, while she was on a space station in the Xik'en dimension, she'd met a bright young woman who had reminded her so much of Rica, and had vowed to her-self to make more time for her family in general and her sisters in specific. She had managed to make more time for them in the months that had followed, even despite her time off-world. As soon as she'd arrived back on her own Earth, she had made a point of making a date with Rica.

Cassidy smiled as she entered the food court proper. Nothing smelled quite like familiarity. It was something she'd learned on her travels to other parts of this world as well as to other worlds: nothing smelled quite like the food of home. The food court was full of local restaurants producing fresh bread, baking pizzas, slicing sandwiches, and brewing fresh coffee. There were several large chains as well, but they couldn't compete for her business or for her olfactory sensations.

She turned, near the edge of the seating area now, and tried to find where Rica had been seated. Was she still lined up for food? A quick scan of those standing told her no.

A large group of tweens stood up at once and started to walk towards the exit, clearly a group of school-age kids that were nearing the end of their lunch break. She wondered how many of them she'd be seeing in her classroom in the next few years. They dispersed, and as they parted she finally caught sight of Rica, seated on the far end of the food court away from her. Her back had been turned to Cassidy, the barest sliver of her round cheek visible.

She was talking to a man.

He was older than Rica by far, closer to Cassidy's age if not actually her age. He was broad and had dark black hair that fell into his eyes the way a pop-singer's did in all their promotional photos. He was wearing a tight black shirt that accented his frame and made him look even paler than he naturally was, and jeans. He had one boot up on the chair across from Rica and had the weight of his arms leaning against his knee. His boots were the thick-soled kind like her own, the sort that were gotten from army surplus outlets. His were black.

Despite his aggressive posture, looming over the sitting Rica, he was smiling warmly. He was laughing at something she'd said, and in that moment Cassidy could not tell if the laugh was fake or genuine.

Cassidy squinted. She could tell from the push of her sister's cheek that she was smiling. She started to make her way past the crowd and through the winding grid of tables to get to them.

The man in black looked up and locked eyes with her, and she stopped dead in her tracks for a moment. There was something uncanny about him staring at her that caused her to pause. They were pinned between each other like that, and time around them seemed to stop.

Then he broke the spell, suddenly, by turning back to Rica and nodding a goodbye before turning his back on her completely and walking away from the food court.

"Hey, wait!" Cassidy called. She found her legs again and started to weave her way through the tables and over chairs to catch him.

Rica turned around at the sound of her sister's voice. "Cassidy?"

The man in black stepped away from the court and down a long hallway that Cassidy knew led only to a maintenance area. There was no escape that way, and she found herself grinning, though she wasn't sure why.

She stepped past Rica, whose gaze turned to follow

her.

"Cassidy, what are you doing?"

Cassidy turned the sharp corner leading down the long hallway to the maintenance area and found... nothing. Just a long, empty hallway with no doors or windows until the very end. She paused, her smile fading and that familiar uptick of her pulse that got her blood moving subsiding. She stood in the mouth of the hall for a moment, as if expecting the stark white walls to produce his black-clad from thin air. She let out a long sigh.

"What is wrong with you?" Rica said, laughing as she met her sister and followed her gaze down the corridor.

"Who was that guy?" Cassidy asked, her tone more serious than even she had expected it to be. She swallowed, controlling herself.

"Just some guy. He said he liked my bag while he was waiting in line at the taco stand."

"Was he hitting on you?"

"What? Ugh. No," Rica warbled. She thought about it for a moment, the idea planted in her head now, then shook it away again. "No, it wasn't like that. He was sweet."

"A lot of older guys pretend to be sweet."

"It was... avuncular," Rica said, finding the word with the same gusto with which Cassidy found artifacts.

Cassidy turned to her, eyebrow raised. "That's a word."

Rica grinned. "There wasn't anything going on, I swear. People can just talk to me, you know."

Cassidy's mouth warbled, and she realized that she was not winning this argument. Reluctantly, she agreed to put it to bed, and they went back to the food court to get a meal of Yackko's Tacos, on Cassidy. They enjoyed the rest of their meal, talking about school and university and summer jobs, and before long the normalcy of it all eroded away the strangeness of the way the exchange had begun.

Without either of them seeing, the man in black named Tallis stepped out of the long hallway, found them with his gaze, then turned and left the mall.

CHAPTER THREE

Every time she stepped into Gamgee's lab, Cassidy felt a sense of wonder.

She hadn't the first time, all those months ago, because she hadn't known exactly what the lab had represented. The first time she'd entered, on Gamgee's invitation, it hadn't felt like taking the first steps into the lab were also taking the first steps into adventure. Now she knew it was, and that knowledge in the back of her head always brought with it a certain tingle of anticipation: what would happen next?

This time, that feeling turned to ash in her mouth as her eyes adjusted to the light from outside and revealed the lab to be torn apart. The smile faded from her face as her eyes found Gamgee, fighting with a fire extinguisher to put out a blaze happening inside his control panel. The extinguisher sputtered, and he cursed a word she'd never heard him say before.

"Gamgee!" she exclaimed, crossing the room in great running leaps. She took the extinguisher from him, primed it, then braced its base between her legs and took aim at the base of the flame with the nozzle. She fired a steady stream of white foam that doused it totally, ending the threat, then let the extinguisher fall to the floor.

She huffed, both their breaths laboured as they took in lungfuls of burning, plasticy air. She turned around the lab slowly now that the immediate danger was done, allowing herself to take in the totality of the destruction. Her first thought when she'd seen it all was that it had been an explosion – that Gamgee had been testing some fantastical device she'd brought back from another world, only to have had it blow up in his face. Now that the danger was less clear and present, she saw immediately that that was not and could not be the case – the destruction was too random, some things thrown away from them and some things towards, some to the left of where the fire had been, and some to the right. The pattern was too random to be anything but human design.

His filing cabinets were on their sides, looking as though someone had pried them open with a crowbar. Whoever had done it hadn't even bothered to go at it from the front and pry open each drawer – they had ripped open the whole side of it, opening it like a turkey and unveiling its innards. Several of his computers were smashed, both the towers and monitors. The towers she understood, but all smashing the monitors did was scatter plastic and liquid crystal everywhere. The monitors told her that, on some level, whomever had done this had revelled in the destruction.

Gamgee's desk projector – which he used to display the maps to the locations he sent her to in 3D – had taken the most damage. The entire surface of it was smashed, and even now it was attempting to display a security warning but it was so cracked and garbled that only a few pixels of it floated in the air above – so few that she hadn't even noticed them until she started looking for them.

"Thank you," Gamgee said, finally catching his breath and fixing his glasses back up onto his nose. "I hate those things."

"What happened here?"

"We've had an intruder," Gamgee said matter-of-factly. He nodded to the security camera in the far corner of the ceiling and pulled his tablet out of his bag as he spoke to her. It started booting up.

"Did they get anything? Any of the artifacts?" Her voice was suddenly panicked. She thought of the vial of cold-infected dream dust she'd taken from Cephalon, and how it had almost become an incurable, deadly version of itself. The cold-infused dream dust, in the wrong hands, could be devastating and she felt the colour drain from her cheeks as she considered the consequences of it. Consequences that would, ultimately, be her own fault.

Before he could answer, she made her way to one of the locked refrigeration units where they kept the sample and started trying her code.

"I'll know in just a moment," Gamgee said, the tablet having finally booted up and now loading his security feed from the secure server.

Cassidy ignored him, trying desperately instead to remember and input a four-digit code she never used. She slipped twice, and on the third time got it, hearing the lock slide out, and she pulled on the handle.

The sample was there, the blue powder resting comfortably in its tube. It glowed just from the shaking of her opening the fridge, and she breathed a sigh of relief.

"Got it," Gamgee said, even as the recorded sounds of the lab's destruction started to play over the tablet's speakers. There were crashes and grunts as whomever was doing it – a male, by the voice – pushed over the filing cabinet and bisected it and began spilling its files out into the air.

Cassidy walked back up to where Gamgee was standing, slower now. It was less urgent now that she knew the dream dust was safe. She stepped up beside him and looked over his shoulder at the security feed, and suddenly her mouth was dry.

The man on the feed was the man who had been talking to Rica at the mall – dark hair tossing about through the effort of his actions, black shirt, and big, thick black military boots. As if to confirm, he ran his crowbar along the table projector and then carried the motion through to look up at the security camera, meeting her gaze through the gap of time between them just as they had locked eyes in the mall. He was sneering, but there was a smile peeking at the corners of his lips – he was angry, but he was enjoying this.

"I know him," Cassidy said, her voice hushed. She sounded upset in a way she never did, and it got Gamgee's attention and made him raise a bushy eyebrow at her. "I saw him at the mall today, flirting with Rica."

Gamgee winced and looked like he was about to object to that assessment of the situation, then thought better of it. "You're sure it's the same person?" he said.

Cassidy watched as the man broke eye contact with

the camera, then turned and used the bar to crack open Gamgee's desk and pull out the drawers. "Very sure."

As they watched, the man in black pulled a small box out of Gamgee's desk and opened it. He took something out, a small metal stick that looked similar to a USB drive, and examined it. He smiled, so broadly that Cassidy could see the skin of his cheeks push up even from the side.

He turned and held the device up to the camera, smiled at them, and saluted. He put it safely into his pocket, picked up his crowbar again, then continued his destruction.

"What was that?" Cassidy asked. The device had looked familiar, but the grain on the feed made it hard to tell exactly what it had been.

"The Digital Heart," Gamgee frowned. "He took the Digital Heart you brought back from Dead World."

CHAPTER FOUR

Preston Cane was slow to pack anything into his overnight bag. He was always slow at things he was told to do or had to do: it was one of the great flaws of him. Even as her sisters were making sure they'd packed their toiletries and zipping up, Preston Cane was still deciding between the merits of tube socks versus no-shows.

Cassidy huffed, marching over to him. "Stop it, that doesn't matter." She snatched the tube socks from his hand and shoved them into his bag with force. "You're just going to the hotel. Have fun, relax by the pool, have a drink. Don't... don't think too much about it."

"Can you at least tell me which hotel we're going to?" he asked, warbling. "Or how many pairs I'll need?"

She frowned and reached into his dresser drawer and scooped up a handful of socks and shoved them all in.

He regarded her cautiously, but nodded.

"That's actually a good point," Margo said, stepping into the doorway with her bag over her shoulder. Rica was in the hall behind her. "Where the hotel is really dictates what I'm taking. Like, if it's the one outside the city limits,

I'm definitely bringing my swim gear, but if it's the one with the outlet mall attached, forget that."

"It's..." Cassidy started with a whispered hiss, then stopped herself, eyeing the corners of the room as though there were ears waiting and listening in on what she was about to say. She stopped. When she spoke again her voice was sterner, yet more defeated. "Just get your things ready, please."

Margo raised an eyebrow, then turned back to Rica. She patted her bag. "We are ready... what's up?"

"Nothing," she frowned, getting several of her father's shirts from the closet and then bringing them to his bag and laying them in, folded. "Just... get your things. And where's Mom?"

"I texted her. She's finishing up at the Farmers' Market, she'll be back soon," Margo said. She shrugged and stepped out of the doorway towards the hall to collect her pool shoes, just in case they were being put up in the hotel outside the city.

Rica stopped Cassidy, putting out a hand so that it caught her sister by the crook of her arm as she walked by. "You said you wanted to be closer," she said, her voice level and matter-of-fact, speaking more like Cassidy than herself for a moment. She spoke as though she were channelling wisdom from beyond her years. "Being closer means being honest."

Preston and Margo both stopped what they were doing and turned from Rica to Cassidy.

Cassidy frowned, pursing her lips. "You know that work I've been doing for Dr. Gamgee?"

They nodded.

"It's not always... safe. I know that a lot of what I've done in my life hasn't been strictly 'safe,' but sometimes this work has the potential to get very, very unsafe." She paused, waiting for them to ask questions. When none came, she continued. "Last night there was a break-in at his office. Some guy... he trashed the place. He stole something I'd recovered on an expedition. Something we were still... cataloguing."

Rica tilted her head, catching the hesitation and knowing that it meant her sister wasn't being totally forthright with her, but deciding that whatever bit she was holding back wasn't salient to the story. Being honest didn't always mean giving everything. "And?"

"On the security footage... it was the guy you met at the mall. The older one that was flirting with you."

Preston stopped what he was doing and turned to Rica with eyebrows raised to their apex. Margo did the same. "Pardon?"

"He wasn't flirting," Rica insisted. Then she let it go, that wasn't the point. "You're sure it was him? Not just your brain filling in missing details with someone else you just saw?"

"I'm sure. Dark hair, coming down in front of his face like an anti-hero from a manga. Dark shirt, jeans, athletic. Strong jaw, my height."

Margo bobbed her eyebrows. "Are we sure we don't want him to have been flirting?"

"This is serious," Cassidy stressed. "It's not a coincidence that he was at the lab and around you. That's a Venn diagram with not a lot of overlap: it's basically me. So we need to assume he's messing my life up for some reason and get you guys to–"

"I met a young man the other day that fit that description," Preston interrupted, his voice hollow and far away. "He seemed nice."

Cassidy stared at him. "You see? This isn't okay. We've got to get to the hotel now. And I don't want to say which one, just on the off-chance... that he's listening. Somehow." They stared at her. She huffed. "You're not being paranoid if somebody really is out to get you."

Rica frowned at that logic for a moment, then reluctantly nodded. She stepped into the room to help her father get the last of his clothes ready. Margo joined as well.

"Thank you," Cassidy smiled, letting out a sigh. She pulled her phone out of her pocket and started to dial. "Now we just need to figure out where Mom is."

She put the phone to her ear and listened to it ring. A few seconds later, on the nightstand, her mother's ringtone called out to them. All four of them turned to stare at it.

***

Kayla Cane walked through the lanes at the Plainsfield Farmers' Market with a wide smile on her face. She had just found the perfect tomato: round and firm, and about the size of a baseball. It was so perfect she almost didn't want to use it later, but would.

Walking in time with her, several feet behind, was a tall man with dark hair and a dark shirt. He had a strong jaw, and his eyes followed Kayla wherever she went.

CHAPTER FIVE

"Excuse me?" Tallis asked, stepping up behind Kayla and putting a gentle hand on her shoulder. "I think this was yours." He held out a gold necklace to her, its chain wrapped around each of his lanky fingers for stability.

The necklace was one that she'd been looking at a moment before, at a table several slots away. The vendor was a jeweller that made pieces by trapping flowers in resin – her booth was lined with dead foliage, contained in suspended animation at the moment of their demise, each petal smoothed out until it blossomed for whomever came near. This one in particular was a Lithodora, the starkness of its deep blue faded by the resin it was encased in, but the yellow at its centre as bright as the midday sun.

Kayla stared at it for just a moment, then smiled and turned her kind eyes towards the man. She noticed the strange jewelry along the side of his face – shimmering gold, with small crystals. It was hard to turn away from the necklace to look at him, actually. The piece had called her so readily when she'd been at the booth that it had been a struggle to turn away from it. She'd wondered –

and not for the first time – what it was in humans that
called them to certain objects, especially when there was
little logic in the exchange. She had touched it, even, but
then stepped away from it. Despite the strange pull it had
on her, she knew that it was frivolous.

She stared at it now again, at how the light caught the
edge of the resin and yet also lit the flower within. "No,"
she said finally, forcing herself to look past it to the man
holding it. He transfixed her for a moment, too. "I didn't
drop that, I'm sorry."

"I didn't say you dropped it, I said it was yours," he
said, his voice smooth like silk. He stepped around to be
behind her, asking permission with his motion, and she
nodded. He placed the necklace around her, clasping it
with deft fingers. It was even the right size, hanging below her collarbones and looking like it had always been
there. He stepped back around to see it on her, like an art-
ist admiring his work. "There, you see? I knew it. Yours."

She touched its edge again, just as she had when she'd
been admiring it, then stepped back to the mirror that the
vendor had set up. It did look perfect on her, just as she'd
imagined it would. There were some things in life that
disappointed – that never looked the same on the rack as
they did in real life: jeans, shoes, and shirts with full-body
prints – but this was exactly the same on as it had been
in her mind's eye. She stared at it and the reflection of
her with it for a long moment, as though seeing herself
complete for the first time. Tallis was behind her and she
could see his reflection over her own shoulder. "Really, I
shouldn't," she protested one last time, but without con-
viction.

"Please," he said, and she heard his voice become unsteady despite his smile. "I saw it and saw you looking at it and I knew that it was meant to be yours. Please."

Kayla smiled, then nodded and stepped away from the mirror.

Tallis smiled at her for a long moment, then a startled expression came over him as though he had become aware that he might have let the moment linger too long. He coughed into his fist then turned and motioned to the market. "It's a lovely place. And a lovely day for it. Do you come here often?"

"I do," Kayla smiled. "I used to come with my children, although my oldest hated it."

"I can't imagine that's true."

"Ooooh, it is. She used to beg and scream to be free of it. It got to the point that I'd try bribing her with treats or food or toys from the vendors, but she wouldn't have it. When she got old enough I started leaving her home with her books instead."

Tallis shook his head, smiling.

"Did they have Farmers' Markets where you're from...?"

His smile faded for a moment, and when it returned it was a wistful smirk. "Yes, actually. They did. I used to enjoy going to them with my mother very, very much. When she was alive."

"Do they have butt-kicking where you're from?" came a voice from behind them. "Because if not, I'd be happy to introduce you to the concept."

Tallis turned, revealing that Cassidy had stepped up behind them. Her shoulders were already squared and ready, her body tilted towards him to make her frame as small a target as possible if he chose to strike. His smile widened as he saw her, travelling totally up one side of his cheek. "Why hello."

"Cassidy?" Kayla asked, confused. "What're you doing here?" She noticed her daughter's aggressive stance and recognized it from years of karate training. "What's going on?"

"Get out of here, Mom," Cassidy said, not taking her gaze away from Tallis for an instant to regard her. She stared at the Branch of Languages that ran along his cheek and recognized it for what it was and what it meant, and some of the colour drained from her. "Go back to the house. Dad's waiting for you."

"What're you—"

"I know what this must look like," Tallis cooed, putting both his hands up with palms open in a 'calm down' gesture that could have all too easily become aggressive at a moment's notice. "But I swear, there's nothing sinister happening here."

"Who is this?" Kayla asked, stepping back away from both of them.

"He destroyed Gamgee's lab," Cassidy said matter-of-factly. "Stole something. He's been after me, and he was stalking Rica and Dad."

Kayla turned to him, sympathy transforming completely into anger in one fell swoop. "You did what?"

Tallis turned away from Cassidy, the angered glare seeming to shake him. He pursed his lips and turned back, now glaring with new anger at Cassidy. "This isn't what it looks like. I'm not 'after you.'"

"You could have fooled me."

He sighed. "Why don't you ask Gamgee why I was there?"

"You were there for the Digital Heart."

"No. Yes... but, no." He smirked. He was starting to enjoy this, and started to step around her in a wide circle. She adjusted her stance towards him in increments, always keeping the smallest part of herself facing him.

"How'd you find me?"

"Actually, I have a better question. Because the answer to it also answers the 'why I was at Gamgee's lab' question, and I like it when one thing answers two questions. I like the symmetry of it. It always seems... planned. So here it is: how... did he find you?"

Cassidy stopped turning to meet him, the unexpected question shaking her a little. She stiffened, breaking her stance. "What do you mean?"

He stopped stepping around her, smiling. He was a full one-hundred and eighty degrees from where he had started, in relation to her. "I mean exactly that. How did Gamgee find you? Every question you have, that question also answers. That is the whole thing."

"Then tell me it."

He smiled. "It'll be better if it comes from him." He said the last word with venom in his voice, then turned quickly and ran towards the exit. It was only then that Cassidy realized that he had circled her until he was closer to it than she was.

"Dang it!" she hissed, then started after him.

"Cassidy, stop!" her mother yelled.

She did so, turning back to her, wedged between the

two forces pulling her for a long moment. After only an instant or two of hesitation, the waiting made her choice for her, as Tallis' lead and steady run made the gap between them insurmountable. She cursed through her teeth, then turned back to her mother.

"Take this," she said, slapping her own phone into her mother's hands. "Call Dad; you left your phone at the house. Don't let him off the line the whole time until you join him, just in case something happens."

"What was that about?" Kayla demanded, gripping the bobble on the end of her necklace as though it were now a talisman.

"I don't know," Cassidy admitted, lowering her eyes at Tallis as he vanished from view. "But I am going to find out."

CHAPTER SIX

Cassidy slammed her hands down on the broken projection table in Gamgee's office, making him jump and strike his head on it from underneath. The attack had shorted out the mechanism underneath that made the entire thing function, and he had been desperately trying to repair it when she'd come in. She'd never taken note of it before, but it looked as though there were ARC crystals helping run the mechanism.

"How did you find me?" she asked, her tone sharp and accusatory.

He rubbed his bald head and grunted as he pulled himself out from under the table. "Pardon?"

"I met the man who did this today," she said, motioning to the destruction around her. "He was following my mother. Who knows what would have happened if I hadn't shown up."

"Nothing would have happened."

"He was wearing a Branch of Languages, Gamgee," Cassidy stressed. "And he told me to ask you how you found me. He said that that would answer all my questions, even the ones I hadn't asked yet."

Gamgee stared at her for a long moment, rubbing his head to dull the pain of his bruise at first and then moving down to stroke the back of his neck in a move she'd rarely seen him do: one that displayed anxiety. He frowned, clearing his throat. "You weren't the first adventurer I worked with. The first person who hopped between worlds for me."

Her eyebrows raised and the colour left her cheeks. She felt her jaw work itself into a tight hinge and felt her palms resting on the broken glass of the projector curl up into fists, but she said nothing. She stared at him, waiting for him to continue without giving him the satisfaction of beckoning him to.

"Some time ago now, I was approached by a young man who said he was from another world. He called himself Tallis. I thought he was crazy." Gamgee smirked a little. "He was young and he was brash, and I thought the whole thing was a scam, honestly. But the more I talked to him... the more I started to believe it. That there could be holes between worlds." He stared wistfully off into the distance for a moment, remembering what it was like to discover that truth for the first time. "He told me that he'd found me because he'd come from a world where my life was different. Where I'd become a biologist, and not a physicist. A world where I'd cured McMillon disease."

She swallowed, straightening. "You didn't bring back the cure?"

"No, but I did discover it. Not in this reality, but it was 'me.' I took some solace in that when I was accepting my accolades and credit and praise. It was me, just a different version of me."

"He's not from that world, though. The one I went through. His English was too perfect to be the product of the Branch of Languages."

"No, we found that world later. It had an even better adaptation of the cure. It's timeline was more accelerated than ours, it's civilization had started earlier. They were further ahead in some medical breakthroughs than us, so when we found it we adapted their cure into the one Tallis had brought from the other me." He smiled. "He thought only I could understand my own work enough to reverse engineer it. He was right."

She did not smile back at him. "What happened then?"

Gamgee stared at her for a long moment, then swallowed. "Then... he decided to stay. His world wasn't a home to him anymore, but he had this device," Gamgee motioned to his wrist watch, "that he'd picked up on another world that could let him know where other portals were. Together we mapped out... most of the portals that we know the locations of."

Cassidy looked up at where the projection of the map usually hovered, as if expecting it to be there upon mention even though the screen was broken.

"We worked together, just like you and I did. Getting technology and cures and information from other worlds that could help us, here. Everything was fine... until one day, he went through a portal and didn't come back."

Cassidy swallowed, locking eyes with him. "What did you do?"

"Nothing. I'd... assumed, honestly, that he'd moved

on. That he'd found another world to call home, or that he'd just grown tired of the chase. He and I didn't have the same relationship we do, it was always strained. Always hard. We bickered, a lot. When he didn't come back, I'd assumed he'd had enough of it."

Cassidy nodded, looking away and thinking about this. She squinted. "What was he looking for?"

"Hm?"

"What was he after, the last time you saw him?"

Gamgee turned back to the opaque crystals that helped run the projector he was trying to fix. "ARC crystals."

Cassidy's jaw went slack. "You abandoned him on Xik'en? A planet that's hostile to mammals? To humans?"

"I didn't know that, then." He sighed.

"He wasn't in retirement, he'd probably spent all that time rotting in an Xik'en prison cell!"

"I didn't know that, then," he reiterated.

She squinted. "But you knew it when I came back. When I came back from the Bermuda Triangle portal and gave my report, you knew it then. You knew what that world was like and what probably happened there and you chose not to tell me or do anything about it, even then."

Gamgee pursed his lips in shame, then nodded.

Cassidy cursed, turning away from him and placing her hands on her hips. She stayed like that for a long time, then turned to face him from over her shoulder. "That doesn't explain how you found me."

CHAPTER SEVEN

Tallis sat among the discarded circuitry and technology of his workspace, sparks illuminating his stark features as he soldered a new wire into the board in front of him. It was long and green, with several rows of transistors lining one side that he'd placed to feed back from the current and through a rewired USB port he had attached to the side opposite him. There was a second on the side closest – this one a micro-USB – that fed out into a series of uninsulated wires. Those wires travelled in a spiral around his arm and came to a head connected into the glowing wristwatch he had on his left arm.

He made several adjustments to the soldering, keeping the screen of his watch for any warning signs as he did, but nothing had illuminated it yet.

The chair he was on had been salvaged from a scrap yard, as had many of the circuit boards and screens and terminals. There was a mattress on the floor behind him with no blankets or bedding on it, not that any was needed: the basement he was in was hot. He sweated at night, surrounded by the teetering towers of technology. The home he was in was vacant and for sale, and had been on the market for quite some time. Nobody would notice him there, but he couldn't risk being upstairs in case a nosey neighbour saw him through the window and called the owners or the police.

The chair was not comfortable and neither was the bed, but both were far and above more comforting than a Xik'en penitentiary, and so he had slept some of the best, more restful sleeps of his life. The Xik'en, he had come to learn, were not believers in 'reform' when it came to mammals: only incarceration and punishment.

He soldered the last wire in place, and suddenly the screen on his watch came to life. It cycled through all the different colours it could make – red, green, blue, yellow, and purple – before doing them all again and settling on its "default positive" of red for a moment. He smiled. He didn't understand this world, where green meant something positive. His screen flashed red, meaning it had accepted the wiring, and he smiled.

Tallis reached into his pocket and produced the Digital Heart. He carefully plugged it into the wires coming from the altered USB slot on the side away from him and turned back to the screen.

He looked at another screen to his right. It showed a digital map of Plainsfield, and a blinking light that read Cassidy on the dot that represented a hotel on the edge of the city.

As if by magic, the firmware of the Digital Heart interacted with that of the alien device and started to repair it. He watched it flicker through diagnostics, ones and zeros fluttering over the screen as it improved itself based on the Heart's base programming, and he smiled.

When it was done he pressed a button on either side of the watch at once, and this time when the screen lit up it projected a small hologram into the air above his wrist. He swiped through the air of it and found that he could interact with it again, like a smartphone, and grinned.

He scrolled through his apps until he found the call feature, then selected Gamgee's name from the list of contacts.

***

Cassidy cursed, turning away from him and placing her hands on her hips. She stayed like that for a long time, then turned to face him from over her shoulder. "That doesn't explain how you found me."

There was a loud beeping sound from under the table then, and the few projection lights that were still working started to sputter to life.

Gamgee turned and stepped over to the exposed terminal, where the ARC crystals were glowing to life.

"What's happening?" Cassidy asked, stepping up to the screen as an image started to form.

"Someone's calling."

"It can accept calls?"

As if in answer, Tallis appeared in a blue projection hovering over the table. There were spots of him missing as not all the projection bulbs were functioning, but it seemed as though something on Tallis' side was working to compensate for that. He was much larger than he should have been, only his bust visible and appearing at close to five times his actual size.

"Hello, can you hear me?" Tallis said. The giant figure reached out and tapped something in front of him, and the entire image shimmered and fluttered away and produced a blunt -tunk tunk- sound. "I can't see you or hear you, but that makes sense. I'm assuming you can see me."

Gamgee stepped up close to the shimmering blue giant, his mouth agape.

"I met the new version. She's nice, she's got spunk, I've gotta say. Nothing wrong with how she was raised, I'll say that."

"Why is he talking about me like that?" Cassidy asked.

"He doesn't know you're here. My setup isn't set up to make calls, he's just hacked into the projection system. Like when you video call someone that doesn't have a camera or microphone attached."

"You guys do good work," Tallis continued, licking his lips. "And you should keep doing good work... but not off of my blood, sweat, and tears, Gamgee." He paused. "I want my work, Gamgee. And all the work that's come from my work. Fruit of the poisonous tree, and all that. I deserve it all, and I want it all. In fact I'd like you to meet me at Plainsfield Park today at five to produce it. You'll know the spot." He stopped for a moment, then smiled magnanimously. "I have no desire to shut you down. This is not about revenge," he said, in a tone that left no doubt that it was, mostly, about revenge. "I just want to start up on my own, like I would have if I hadn't met you. I want you out of my life, want to start fresh." He frowned, then reached for the screen again. "And if you don't, I'll burn your whole world down to get it. I'm sorry. See you at five."

The projection blinked off, and all of the lights that still worked around the table disengaged.

"He wants all the work," Gamgee said, his voice hushed. "His work and everything based on it? That's everything. He wants to take everything from me."

Cassidy laughed ruefully. "I mean it doesn't sound like you don't deserve it. Lying. Keeping secrets. Leaving a man in a Xik'en prison. These don't sound like things people do when they don't want their work taken from them."

Gamgee turned on her. "You don't know what you're saying. He's not like me, Cassidy. We fought, often and always. He doesn't want the research to help mankind – he wants money. When he brought the cure for McMillon disease, he wanted to patent it, charge for it. Not a lot... not an insane, ten-thousand percent markup... but enough that he would have been one of the richest men in the world."

Cassidy looked around the large laboratory. "You seem to have done alright for yourself."

"Off grants. Off awards. And all of it, you'll notice, right back into the project. If I give him everything, that all changes. All of it."

She paused for a long moment, lips still tight. She was still angry with him. She nodded.

CHAPTER EIGHT

Tallis stood in the middle of the open field portion of the Plainsfield Park, people playing Frisbee and catch all around him. He stood in one spot and never swayed, like a high tower in an open field, the energy of the evening park happening all around him. It was chaos, but a controlled chaos, and he watched it all with a warm smile on his face as people ran and yelled and laughed. All the while, they ignored him. It was like he wasn't even there.

The Branch of Languages hugged the side of his jaw and caught the light from the lowering sun, making it shimmer. Despite the fact that it sparkled and vied for attention, nobody paid it any. He remembered, briefly, that on his home world if someone had worn something so plainly audacious it would have earned them stares and glares and ridicule. He wondered if the lack of attention the Branch was being paid was due to the changes that made this dimension unique... or simply the natural passage of time and the increased acceptance of different things.

It occurred to his wandering mind that many, many

years had passed since he had last stepped foot on his 'own' Earth, and that in the time since, things might have changed. Culture would have changed, and trends and fads. Politics would have certainly changed, both on a micro level and a broader, global level. It was entirely possible that, given the changes and the time he'd been away, there was no longer any Earth that would feel familiar to him. That 'home' was something he would only ever be able to feel again in nostalgia.

"You were on the call as well, I take it?" he said, a slow smirk growing over his features. He turned around and his gaze found Cassidy, who had been approaching from behind him from across the field. She was now ten feet away, and stopped suddenly when he laid eyes on her. There was something about his eyes that made her pull to a stop, every time.

"I was," she said definitively.

He chuckled humourlessly, looking up at the sky. "I should have known. I tracked your phone and I thought – I thought – that, given the perceived threat to your family, that you'd stay with them. Comfort them, give them hugs and normalcy... but I should have known better, shouldn't I have? Of course you were with Gamgee. I don't know how I thought you'd be anywhere else."

She paused, her step hesitant. When she took another step towards him he made one away, his first.

"Gamgee told me what you want to do with the research," she said in a matter-of-fact tone. "You want to exploit it, for profit."

He chuckled. "You're an idealist, I get that. Tell me: when doctors take a pay check for performing a heart transplant, are they being exploitative? Hm? What about grocery clerks, stocking shelves? Are they exploiting the people who pay them?"

"That's not the same."

"You seem to think it is. You seem to want to paint a picture where getting paid a proper rate for my work is wrong, when really it incentivizes me to do more of my work. If my work is valuable to mankind then they should pay me for the pleasure, as simple as that."

"Some things, sure. That bobble on the side of your face," she motioned along the side of her own face to indicate the Branch of Languages on his. "But not things like cures for diseases. Not things like the McMillon disease cure."

Tallis laughed ruefully, but there wasn't joy in it. She thought she might have even saw tears forming in his eyes before he pushed them away. "Because you care about your family. Your father."

She straightened. "Yes."

"Your family that you never see. You're always out on your adventures – on other worlds, other planets, other dimensions – never once back here. Not long enough to see what's happening." He licked his lips. "How far was your father along into Stage Two before you noticed?"

She balked and swallowed, but said nothing.

"Or did you have to be told to notice? You spend so little time with them. Rica, she's grown up while you weren't even looking, and now you'll never get those years back. She's going to the same university you teach at, but I bet she doesn't want you to let anyone know about your connection."

"She wants to make it on her own merit," Cassidy snapped, forgetting herself and then recomposing herself.

"She's had to get by on her own merit, thus far, because you weren't there. Now she doesn't want you involved at the tail end. She's made it all this way without your help, without you being there, why would she want you stamping your name on the credit now, after all this time?"

Cassidy's eyebrows furrowed. She thought for a long moment, then shook her head. "It's not like that."

He met her eyes. "Don't pretend it's not. You chase the thrill, I know the type. I was the same. Not much excuse to get your blood pumping at Family Game Night, so why bother, right?"

"I went to Family Game Nights every week while Rica and Margo were growing up, thanks."

"But were you really there?" he squinted. "Were you there in your head? Or were you off somewhere else, your mind on some adventure while you tapped the piece along the board like a zombie?"

Cassidy nodded, pursing her lips and swallowing. "I'm sorry about what happened to you on Xik'en," she said, changing the topic with confidence in her voice. "I really am. That place was awful. I only survived it because I had a friend there. I can't imagine what it would have been like to have been there without one."

Tallis' lip curled. "You don't deserve them, you know. The friends. The family. You don't appreciate them and they stick by you and they will until it's over, but you don't deserve them." His pale cheeks were growing red and hot.

"You seem like you're getting angrier at me than you are at Gamgee."

He paused, considered that with a sneer on his face, then nodded. "That is... accurate. Yes."

She thought for a moment, then stepped forward. This time he did not step back. "Maybe you'd like to have it out then? Decide this like adventurers, winner take all?"

"By all, do you mean the research?"

"I do."

"Then. I. Agree." He said each word clipped, like they were each their own sentence. "Where?"

"There's a beach five miles from the outer edge of Plainsfield, with evergreen trees and brush all around it. It continues to the edge of the continent, then suddenly drops off into large, tanned boulders. You've never seen boulders like these. They're laid there like toys a toddler was done playing with. You can hear the waves crash there, can feel the surf against your skin."

"I know the place," he nodded. "Bring the files."

She nodded, and he turned and marched away from her again, but this time she made no effort to catch him, she merely watched him go with a steely resolve in her eyes.

CHAPTER NINE

Cassidy burst through the doors of Gamgee's lab, already running toward the line of locked refrigeration units. Gamgee stood up from his repairs quickly, avoiding striking his head this time, and spun around to watch her. "Cassidy? What are you doing?"

She did not answer, instead finding her way to the third fridge in and trying her four-digit code. She got it on the first try and pulled the door open to the hiss of air and plumes of cold condensation.

The sample was there, the blue powder resting comfortably in its tube. It glowed just from the shaking of her opening the fridge, and she stared at it with a stern, resigned expression.

It was the cold-infected dream dust from Cephalon.

Gamgee's face lost colour and he took a step towards her. "What are you planning on doing with that?"

"What I have to."

CHAPTER TEN

Tallis followed the tracks that had been left in the tall grass before him, leading away from the crumbling road and the dense plot of evergreen trees and down to the very edge of the continent, suddenly dropping off into large, tanned boulders. They came together haphazardly and yet with great purpose, but most were firmly in place after an age of time and pressure. They formed caves that dotted the shoreline, lined with kelp and small shellfish. The tide was out, but it was clear that at another day or time the caves might have been hip deep with crashing waves.

On the air he could hear the steady clap of work, like thunder on the open air. There would be a large snap, and then several seconds. He knew what it was by the sound of it, but didn't know why it was. He came off the steep boulders onto the relative flatness of the shore, a brief edge of ten feet that bordered the last edge of the world before disappearing into the oblivion of the sea. The waves were such a deep blue they were nearly black, like ink pushing its way towards the unspent parchment of the forest. They crashed and rolled, leaving creamy foam in the crevices and cracks of the stone.

There were several caves in the cliffside, holes that came to sharp points at the top and bottom, widening into foot-long gaps at their middles. They gaped like maws, small breaks in reality where light had no place. There were several of them in varying shapes and sizes, some appearing more inhabitable by an adult human form than others. One of them was elevated slightly above the rest, and Cassidy was at its mouth.

She was thick with sweat that covered her face, and had been there so long that it had begun to dry on and have a new layer come in its wake. It was soaked into her shirt under her arms, her jacket off and her suspenders showing. Her mouth was open with the stress and heat of it, and she had a pickaxe in her hands. She was chiselling away at the slender gap of the cave, making it wider and wider. It was where the thunderclap had come from, the pause as she caught her breath, the anticipation between them.

He stepped up to her, slowly, and she saw him coming out of the corner of her eye. She stopped her work, wiped her brow with her bare arm, then opened a bottle of ice water that had been resting at her side. She drank it all, every last bit of it.

"This isn't what I expected to find," Tallis said, slowly closing the gap between them.

She swallowed, then motioned for him to stop and turn around.

There was a bear walking along the edge of a steep ridge of the cliff, its fur barely visible between the trees but clearly there all the same. It ate berries the way only a bear could, entire branches of the bush finding their way into its mouth and then being strained through clenched, sharpened teeth when it pulled back. It ignored them, far enough away that neither party was a danger to the other. It was used to humans. Even this far into the wild, there was no wilderness.

"That is beautiful," he said, admiring it.

"I saw one just like that the first time I was out here," Cassidy mused, stepping away from her work. She slid on her bomber jacket, which had been resting on the stone next to her, and suddenly looked clean.

Tallis raised an eyebrow at her, noticing the lack of bullet holes or scrapes. "New jacket?"

She splayed out her arms and held them aloft, looking from arm to arm as though she were just noticing it for the first time. She had made two stops after she'd gone to see Gamgee, and one of them had been back to the store she had visited right before she saw Tallis for the first time. She had gone back and this time she had taken the coat off the rack without hesitation, marched right to the register and paid for it. Her old, torn coat was back in her car, thrown over the back seat like an animal carcass and with just as many bullet holes in it. This one still smelled of new, the oils in it reaching her nostrils even as she raised them. "Yeah. I thought it was about time."

"Do you have the files?" he asked, his voice losing some of its conversational impishness.

She reached to her breast pocket and unbuckled it, the new clasp coming loose with difficulty. She fished her entire hand in and came back with a thick jump drive, connector cables dangling from it. She kept its front facing him, the symbol of the big tech firm that made it glimmering in the light of the setting sun.

"You expect me to believe that's the only copy?"

"Does it need to be the only copy? Once you patent what's on it, it doesn't matter what we do."

He squinted. "I don't want competition."

"I'll magnetize any copies we have if you win. Which, you won't. So let's not bother arguing about the logistics of how something will work that's never going to happen for too long, okay?"

He smirked. "You know I'm going to win. We always win. And I know that you know I'm going to win... because if you didn't, you wouldn't have brought the drive at all."

She shuffled on her feet, her eyes flitting back to the hole in the rock she had been working at. There was water coming from it, like a small freshwater stream that joined the ocean a little ways down the beach. It was like freshwater, and all logic stated it should be freshwater, but she knew that if she bent and took a mouthful of it, that it would be salt. She did not respond to his taunt, just set her jaw and stared at him.

"So how are we going to do this?" he asked, stepping around her in a slow arc, just as he had at the Farmers' Market. He motioned towards the lapping waves. "Will we fight to the death up to our ankles in sea foam, wrestling and both getting soaked and cold?" He paused and smirked. "That would certainly be dramatic, and I'd be lying if I said I'd never wondered what a fight like that would turn out like."

"That's not really my style," she replied, each word clipped. She had closed her fists until her knuckles were white, her right once wrapped around the frame of the drive.

He stopped walking and regarded her, looking her up and down as if appraising her as a fighter. "It's really not, is it? I can see that you can fight, but you don't actually fight much. How do you get out of all those precarious situations we tend to find ourselves in, if that's the case?"

"My brain, mostly," she grinned. "You should try it, sometime."

"Oh, hoho," he laughed heartily. "I'm quite smart, I'll have you know. Top of my class. Much like you, I'd imagine. Maybe in different areas... but still the top. Still the overachiever, the over-exceller. We're a type."

"If you were smart you wouldn't have come at me through my family."

He stopped at that, his face changing from smugness to slackness, as though the statement had taken him aback. "For that last time, I wasn't coming at you through them."

"It had a funny way of looking like that."

"I lost my family," he said, his voice too cold and hurt for any of it to be lies. "I'm sorry if I was feeling... nostalgic isn't the word, but it's close enough. I miss mine, but that didn't give me the right to intrude on yours. I honestly apologize."

She straightened. She had not expected that. "You come at me through my family to get this intel, and then you apologize?"

"As hard as it might be for you to believe, those two

things were not linked."

She squinted.

He swallowed hard, then motioned back to the surf with a broad gesture. "So, what then? If we're not going to duke it out in the water, where?" He was standing at the sea's edge now, the waves licking at the heels of his thick black boots. "Maybe on those rocks you were chipping away at? We could fight like Kirk and the Gorn on that episode of Star Trek." He paused. "Did they have Star Trek, here? I've never looked."

She nodded.

"Amazing the things that are the same. In two worlds, that one little series ran for forty seasons, even with all the differences between us. That's amazing, when you think about it."

She opened her mouth to correct him, then closed it. It wasn't the point. "We're not going to fight."

"Oh? I don't see how you plan on this ending then. Because I hate to be the person who gives bad news, but I will fight. I will absolutely fight. I will fight you and Gamgee and anyone else he recruits to stand in my way to get the work I'm owed." He stepped toward her, and she stepped back toward the slender cave. Her feet almost slipped on the uneven rock, but she steadied herself. He sighed. "You can't keep putting this off. How will it end then?"

"I told you. I'll do the smart thing," she said, holding up the drive with its front toward him again. "And give you the drive."

Before he could respond she had lobbed it through the air at him, throwing it like an underhand baseball pitch that was intended to be hit. The drive went up and then swiftly back down to earth in a narrow arc, and he knew instinctively that it would come short of him and shatter on the rocks, all his work lost forever.

He dove quickly, reaching out both cupped hands and catching the drive even as Cassidy turned and stepped away from him. The drive fell into his waiting arms and bounced, and he snapped it tight to his chest to stop it from escaping and falling to the stone.

There was a sound of breaking glass, and suddenly his black shirt was streaked with shimmering blue dust. It swirled around him and up onto his face and into his nostrils when he gasped for air. He looked up at her, his eyes wide and somewhere between rage and fright and confusion.

She was standing at the mouth of the cave, with one foot propped up on the rock in front of it like the heroes from the old adventure serials.

Tallis looked down at the drive. On the back of it there had been a glass vial taped that had housed the blue dust that was now all over him and in him, streaking his face. "What is this?" he asked angrily.

"Cephalon dream dust," she said matter-of-factly.

He looked down at it, brushing it off his shirt and only succeeding in spreading it.

"I assume you've been to Cephalon?"

He nodded.

"That dream dust... has been fused with the common cold."

His eyes went wide. "What have you done?"

"It'll kill anyone with an imagination... and you have many faults, but I don't think a lack of imagination is one of them."

He staggered, his feet becoming rubber. "I thought you didn't do violence?"

"I don't," she smirked, then reached into her breast pocket again, producing a second vial. This one looked sturdier, like it was made of thick plastic, and it contained a clear liquid that looked like water. "You've never been to Lotus Lorea, have you?"

His brow furrowed.

"No, I found that one. I've been working, too. This is a small, diluted sample of the Lotus Fountain water. I kept it hidden from Gamgee... now I guess I know why. It cures anything." She looked at the vial, then at him. "Put down the drive."

He coughed, and a cloud of blue came from him that shook him. He glared at her... then put the drive down on the shore at his feet. If they stayed like they were, the tides would take them within minutes. "Give me the potion."

Cassidy smiled, nodded, then turned and brought the vial up high. "Catch!"

She threw it into the cave, its plastic so thick that they heard it bounce, and not break. It bounced twice and he was already on his feet, scrambling up the sharp incline of the shore and into the mouth of the cave.

She stepped down the shore quickly, in a wide circle away from him just as he had with her, so that he could not change tactics and attack her, then scooped up the drive just as the approaching tide was about to take it.

CHAPTER ELEVEN

Tallis came out of the mouth of the cave back out onto the beach, even though he hadn't turned around. He'd ran into the cave after the sample of Lotus Fountain water and halfway through instead of getting closer to the wall he'd started out again. There was a ringing in his ears that he recognized at once was not in his head, but a high-pitched alarm.

Cassidy was no longer on the beach, and the day was brighter than it had been.

He gasped and looked around the beach, quickly examining the glint of every stone for the telltale sheen of plastic. The blue dust still clung to him, getting into the fabric of his shirt and in his hair and holding there.

He found the vial, nestled between two great stones and looking like it had always been there. He scooped it up, the clear liquid inside almost seeming to glow with promise. His thumb immediately started to work the cork out of the top, then he thought better of that. He stepped into the sea and let the crashing waves push around him, knocking the Dream Dust that was on his clothes off into the surf and diluting it beyond use. He dipped his head down into the sea of another world and got clean of it, then pushed himself back through the surface.

He stepped back towards the shore with that ringing in his ears getting louder.

He popped the cork top off the bottle and downed the sample of Lotus Fountain water that Cassidy had tossed away, feeling it tingle against his tongue and his throat as it made its way down. He drank it until it was gone, just in case.

He headed back towards the mouth of the cave.

Just as he was exiting the surf, a flying car appeared over the blind of the cliffside and elevated high into the air, shining a spotlight down onto him. Tallis dropped the empty bottle to the ground as three men in SWAT gear appeared over the ridge with their weapons raised.

Tallis turned from them to the mouth of the cave, knowing he couldn't reach it. He smirked. "Clever."

"Slipstreamer," the lead officer said with contempt, upon hearing Tallis' voice. "Put your hands on your face!"

Tallis' lip curled and he considered correcting the man on his grammar, then thought better of it. He put his hands on the top of his head and, when the officer told him to, lowered himself down to his knees. While he was doing so he kept the cave entrance in sight, and couldn't help but wear a smile on his face.

"Very clever."

CHAPTER TWELVE

Cassidy wedged the thin, flat edge of her pickaxe into the scant crack at the bottom of the boulder next to the cave. She dug down into the sand a little more to give herself some leverage, then placed all her weight on the axe's handle and pushed down.

Her leverage did nothing at first and she screamed from the exertion of it, sweat forming from her every pore and streaming down her cheeks and off of her chin. The beach was hot and this made it hotter, but she could hear the distant sounds of yelling and it pressed her on. Could sound waves travel through the portal? She wasn't sure, but didn't see why not, and the uncertainty egged her on.

She let out a warrior's cry and gave one final heave of exertion, and finally the boulder moved. It rocked up on the axis of the axe at first, seeming to balance there in defiance of gravity and logic, before falling from its perch and tumbling down over to block the path.

She let out a sigh of relief, then fell from the rock elevation where the boulder had been into the sand below, her knees soaking in the last trickles of the stream of water from another world.

CHAPTER THIRTEEN

Cassidy stepped into Gamgee's office in a way she never had before, with a resigned hesitation. He was at the far side, doing repairs on the inverter he'd been working on, and was partially obscured by its frame. She looked from side to side as she stepped towards him, at the panels of tech and cameras and lights that lined the walls, and for the first time it did not look impressive, it looked ominous.

The space was wide and open, cold both in temperature and emotionality, the light off the stainless steel instruments giving it an unearthly clean glow. Echoes were a constant in the space, so although he heard Cassidy enter the building long before she reached him, he'd made no effort to set down his work and address her until she was within five feet of him. When she was, he backed his way out from under the hood of the machine he was working on and forced a smile that she did not return. "You made it back."

"I did, yeah," she said with pursed lips. She took the jump drive with his work on it out of her breast pocket and pressed it down onto the terminal in the centre of the room with force, as though she thought that it would have gotten up and run away if she hadn't. "Would you have done anything for me if I hadn't?"

He looked at her and swallowed, unsure how to respond.

"That's... that's kind of what I thought." She tisked and shook her head.

"For you, I would have," he stressed, trying to sound sincere. "For an adventurer like you, I would have done whatever it took to get you back."

Her mouth became a thin line across her face and she shook her head. "I guess that's the thing, isn't it... no matter how exciting things are now... no matter how much they get my blood pumping... I just don't think these will feel like adventures anymore."

She took her hand off of the jump drive and turned her back on Gamgee, leaving it there and walking away from him.

Her footsteps echoed through the massive, empty hall. When she was halfway to the exit he called out after her: "You'll be back, won't you?"

Cassidy did not turn or respond in any way. She made her way to the exit, and out into the bright, natural light of the sunny day.

CHAPTER FOURTEEN

"Can you pass the mash potatoes?" Preston asked, holding his hand out with the palm up and fingers splayed, ready to receive the bowl.

Cassidy smiled. The way he said 'mash potatoes' instead of 'mashed potatoes,' or any number of other small inflections that were uniquely him, always brought a fresh grin to her face.

She raised the blue swirled bowl of mashed potatoes like a ceremonial offering, then set it down with great weight on his waiting hand.

Everyone around the table laughed: Preston, Kayla, Margo and Rica. Rica laughed especially hard, while Margo seemed like she was just chuckling along. Margo didn't laugh involuntarily, often.

The dining room seemed to have grown since the last time she'd been in it, and become more welcoming. They all fit around it comfortably, passing food and utensils between each other with ease. The home seemed more welcoming than it had in years – for the first time in a long time, there was more of a tug to return to it than there was to the road or to the skies or to another world. For once, that ephemeral pull of destiny was bringing her back home, and she did not fight it.

Kayla sat at the far end of the table, eating edamame that had been drizzled in olive oil and topped with fresh black pepper. "So you're not working with Doctor Gamgee anymore?"

Cassidy turned to her. "No. Not anymore." She smiled.

"You'll have to get back to work here, then. Get a new grant, or something."

"Mom," Rica stressed, reaching out and touching the back of her mother's hand. "Money isn't everything."

Kayla bobbed her eyebrows as though she wasn't sure if that were true, but nodded in reluctant agreement.

Cassidy turned to look at her, only noticing now much Tallis' attitude had mirrored her mother's, in a strange way.

"We always win," Tallis had said, she remembered. And then later: "I lost my family" and "I wasn't coming at you through them."

The colour drained from Cassidy's cheeks, and after a moment Preston noticed and put a concerned hand on her arm. "Cass?"

Her mouth was dry, but she spoke. "You named me, right?"

He raised an eyebrow. "Pardon?"

"You named me?" She raised her gaze to meet his eye. "When I was born, you picked the name?"

"... Yes," he answered, drawing out the word. He looked across the table to Kayla. "We wanted something that meant 'clever.' We wanted you to be clever."

She nodded slowly. She turned to her mother. "What would you have named me if I'd been a boy?"

***

Tallis Cane woke in a holding cell with both arms chained to the solid concrete wall at a ninety degree angle. It was dark and he couldn't see the entire room, but he knew the smell of it, the taste of antiseptic in the back of his throat. There was no furniture or fixtures he could see, just bars along one side of the large cell and concrete walls on every other. It was private and yet as public as a panopticon, with anyone able to look into any corner of the cell at any time. There was a large hole with a grate over it in the centre of the floor, and the entire room sloped slightly towards it. He tried not to think about that fact.

He leaned his head back against the stone and laughed, long and loud, and thought of Cassidy. "Very clever."

ABOUT THE AUTHOR

Matthew LeDrew holds an Honours Degree in English from the Memorial University of Newfoundland with a minor in Anthropology. He has served as a jury member for both the 2018 NLBA awards and the 2020 Arts and Letters Awards. He lives in St. John's, Newfoundland.

He has written twenty-two other novels for Engen Books: the ten book Coral Beach Casefiles series, *The Long Road, Cinders, Sinister Intent, Faith, Family Values, Fate's Shadow, Jacobi Street, Touch Your Nose, Infinity, The Tourniquet Reprisal, Exodus of Angels,* and *Garden of the 8th Circle* the latter four of which with co-author Ellen Curtis.

JD Ryot is the reclusive creator of the *Slipstreamers* series from Engen Books. JD is an avid fan of young adult literature and adventure serials. When asked if they had come to this world through a portal themselves, JD Ryot refused to answer. No record of their birth has ever been found... on this world.